For Robin and Beatrice

Children's Books by Robert Bright

GEORGIE

BY ROBERT BRIGHT

A WORLD'S WORK CHILDREN'S BOOK

Copyright 1944 by Doubleday & Co., Inc. All rights reserved. First published in Great Britain 1960 by World's Work Ltd., The Windmill Press, Kingswood, Tadworth, Surrey
Printed in Great Britain by Clark Constable (1982) Ltd., Edinburgh
SBN 437 28811 0   Reprinted 1982

In a little village in the country there was a little house
which belonged to Mr. and Mrs. Whittaker.

Up in the little attic of this little house there lived
a little ghost. His name was Georgie.

Every night at the same time he gave the loose board on the stairs a little creak

And the parlour door a little squeak

And then Mr. and Mrs. Whittaker knew it was time to go to bed.

And Herman, the cat, he knew it was time to prowl.

And as for Miss Oliver, the owl, she knew it was time to wake up and say "Whoo-oo-oo!"

And so it went, with everything as it should be, until Mr. Whittaker took it into his head to hammer a nail into the loose board on the stairs

And to oil the hinges of the parlour door.

And so the stairs wouldn't creak any more

And the door wouldn't squeak any more

And Mr. and Mrs. Whittaker didn't know when it was time to go to bed any more

And Herman he didn't know when it was time to begin
to prowl any more.

And as for Miss Oliver, she didn't know when to wake up any more and went on sleeping.

And Georgie sat up in the attic and moped.

That was a fine how-do-you-do!

Pretty soon, though, Georgie decided to find some other house to haunt. But while he ran to this house

And then to that house

Each house already had a ghost.

The only house in the whole village which didn't have a ghost was Mr. Gloams' place.

But that was so awfully gloomy!

The big door *groaned* so!

And the big stairway *moaned* so!

And besides Mr. Gloams himself was such a crotchety old man, he came near frightening Georgie half to death.

So Georgie ran away to a cow shed where there lived a harmless cow.

But the cow paid no attention to Georgie. She just chewed her cud all the time, and it wasn't much fun.

Meanwhile a lot of time went by and it rained a good deal

And during the winter it snowed to beat the band

And out in the cow shed Georgie was terribly cold and uncomfortable.

BUT what with the dampness from the rain and the coldness from the snow, something happened to that board on the Whittaker stairs and to the hinges on the Whittaker parlour door.

It was Herman who discovered it and told Miss Oliver. And she woke up with a start.

Miss Oliver flew right over to the cow shed to tell Georgie that the board on the stairs was loose again, and that the hinges on the parlour door were rusty again.

What glad tidings these were for Georgie! He ran home lickety-split.

And so, at the same old time, the stairs creaked again

And the parlour door squeaked again

And Mr. and Mrs. Whit-
taker knew when it was time to
go to sleep again

And Herman, he knew when
to begin to prowl again.

And as for Miss Oliver, she knew when it was time to
wake up again and say "Whoo-oo-oo!"
Thank goodness!